WRONG

WRONG

A novel by
Paige Geernaert

Copyright © 2011 by Paige Geernaert.

ISBN:	Softcover	978-1-4653-8118-7
	Ebook	978-1-4653-8119-4

All rights reserved. No part of this book may be reproduced or transmitted in any form or by any means, electronic or mechanical, including photocopying, recording, or by any information storage and retrieval system, without permission in writing from the copyright owner.

This is a work of fiction. Names, characters, places and incidents either are the product of the author's imagination or are used fictitiously, and any resemblance to any actual persons, living or dead, events, or locales is entirely coincidental.

This book was printed in the United States of America.

To order additional copies of this book, contact:
Xlibris Corporation
1-888-795-4274
www.Xlibris.com
Orders@Xlibris.com
105113

ACKNOWLEDGEMENTS

To my sister Rhiannon, who coloured the lines of my story. My friend Radovan, who helped me come up with a million ways to end my book and pushed me to finish it. My family, who shared my short story with everyone and pestered me to lengthen it into a book. To Cody, who was mature and brave enough to allow me to handcuff him so I could get a cover picture. Finally, to Carly, who took pictures with me and edited them until I was satisfied. Thank you ever so much; this could not have been done without you.

The Story That Started It All . . .

A TALE OF WRONGFUL ACCUSATION

It was a chilly night in December when it happened. I was walking to the bench that I had claimed as my bed when I heard something. Being the curious fifteen year old boy I was, I went towards it. The source of the noise was people, fighting to be specific. Lots of them, all with brightly coloured bandanas in their back pockets; it was a gang fight. From the bush I was hiding behind, I could see the flash of light glinting off of the blade of a knife. Time moved in slow-motion as the guy with the knife stalked towards a small girl that was near the back of the gangs. She didn't even see him coming towards her, and thinking back I could've stopped it. I could've saved her life, probably to the detriment of my own but it didn't matter. It doesn't matter because I didn't do it. She fell to the ground clutching at the dark stain that was spreading across her abdomen, the knife handle jutting almost comically out. A few of the girls screeched as they saw her bleeding on the cement. The guy who stabbed the poor girl was the first of many to flee the scene. The rest scattered afterwards, the shock wearing off to panic as they ran in different directions. Back to their homes where they'd resume life like normal and pretend like nothing happened. Me, I ran towards the girl, hoping to console her in her last moments. Her hands reached up to me, cold as the snow that I had just been sitting in. The blood on her fingers smeared on my arms as I stroked my fingers through her blonde hair. Her lips quivered with an unsaid word. I turned my ear towards her and listened carefully; her last words were "thank-you." Her last breath, a cold breeze in my ear. I had just removed her hands from my arms and placed them next to her when I was bathed in a flashing light.

"Put your hands up!" A loud voice boomed over my thoughts.

I obeyed, hesitantly raising my hands above my head and turning around. A cop car was parked behind me, creating a shadow that stretched along the snow. An officer held a gun pointed at me; why, I didn't know at the time. I remember thinking that all I had done was console her and now I was considered deadly. And that is how I ended up here, in a cold, clammy cell surrounded by people clothed in orange jumpsuits-the only colour in this drab environment. I'm now twenty-five years old and I've spent the last ten years of my life in prison. Not that I mind though; I get three meals a day-even though they're terrible. I get a bed with blankets and showers. I've got to say that even though I was thrown in prison for helping a dying girl, this is the best part of my life. I get out tomorrow, back into the world of cruelty that I've been away from for the past ten years of my life. Given the chance however, I would do it all again.

PROLOGUE

The earliest memory I have is when I was seven.

A tall man in a white coat walked with a crestfallen demeanour to me and my mom. We were explained to then that my daddy wasn't coming back. Ever. My momma was never the same after that. She cried every day and drank until she passed out, usually on the floor. Once, she landed on broken glass. I remember the blood. When I look back it wasn't that much, but to a seven year old, it was a lot. I started doing small chores then for people in my apartment building so that I could escape the darkness my apartment withheld. Mom spent all the welfare cheques on alcohol so it became my job to earn money for myself, which the neighbours happily gave me for helping them. I did this for five years; watching mom drink, cleaning up after her and doing errands for people. I even dropped out of school at ten because it got in the way. What did I get in return? I got kicked out at twelve, that's what. She threw me out on the street because I "took too much money". Are you kidding me? I maybe got five dollars a month from her. *A month!* That's sixty dollars a year from her; that amount of money could hardly buy groceries for a week! But no matter, that's the past now. Like a good boy, I grabbed a plastic bag, put some clothes in, and walked out the door. No goodbye . . . nothing. She just sat at the table with a bottle in hand.

I still did errands for the people who lived in the apartment building, the only difference being that I usually slept on a bench about a block away. Sometimes people would let me sleep on their couches, take a shower and eat. In fact, I almost preferred their housing over money, especially in the cold months. Some of the older ladies whose children had all grown up and moved away even bought me clothes for my birthday or Christmas. They were more of a mother to me than mine ever was. It went on like that for three years. I even got a part-time job at a fast food place so that I could afford to pay someone for their housing. It didn't last long, but I got a good amount of money. Then, my life changed. It was a chilly night in December when it happened. I was making my way over to a bench when I heard a scuffle a little bit away. Fights were common where I grew up, but never this big of a fight. There were a lot more people than normal stomping noisily over the ground. Being the curious fifteen year old boy I was, I went towards the sound. What I saw was chaotic and insane. All of the people had coloured bandannas in their pockets; blue and red. From behind the bushes I saw everything. I saw the seemingly harmless fighting turn into horrible danger. I saw light glint off a metal blade and I tensed as the wielder of the knife walked towards a small girl. Her hand twitched nervously towards her pocket. He strode forward with a sickening grin. In the blink of an eye things had gone from bad to worse.

 I could've saved her if I hadn't sat around like a coward. She could've still been alive to go home to her family. I probably wouldn't be alive if I had, that guy did look terrifying, but it didn't matter. I was a coward and I was too late.

 The man was looking at the blood on his hand in horror, like he had been possessed to kill her. Her bright green eyes flashed up from her abdomen to meet his eyes as her mouth opened in a silent gasp of agony. He turned on his heel and started running clumsily through the mass of people. Shrieks pierced the air and sobs were barely audible over shoes slapping on the ground. All the people ran like frightened children, their harmless games suddenly lethal.

 An unknown urge pushed me towards the girl who had been left alone on the pavement. A dark crimson puddle pooled around her. She had her hands wrapped gingerly around the knife that jutted from her abdomen. The dim light made the knife look so much more sinister than before.

 I learned later on that her name was Mae, not that it made much of a difference.

When I touched her hand her eyes flew open and she started to gasp for breath. I could tell that she was disoriented and fighting with herself. A single tear rolled down her cheek; only one. Her hand rose to grasp my arm, leaving blood in its wake. She tried to say something but it was so quiet that I had to lean over to put my ear near her face.

"Thank-You." Her last words were hardly a whisper against the wind. She coughed, blood splattering on the side of my face. She sighed out her last breath as I folded her hands across her chest.

"PUT YOUR HANDS UP!"

Trembling, I slowly raised my hands and got to my feet. Before I even had time to think, a pair of handcuffs were slapped around my wrists. The cold metal bit into my skin as I was pulled backwards and shoved none too nicely into the back seat of a car.

"You have the right to remain silent. Anything you say can and will be used against you in a court of justice." A harsh voice screamed in my ear.

The door slammed when I clenched my jaw shut.

And that is how I ended up in prison. Although I was wrongfully accused, prison was the best part of my life. I got three meals a day, showers and a bed. Aside from the frightening criminals and no privacy this was the best home I've had so far. Given the chance, I would probably do it again. Although I sometimes curled up in my bunk, attempting to hide from reality. The reality that someone was murdered . . . and I could've stopped it.

MAE'S STORY

"Oh come on. It's just going to be a little rumble. Codie's going . . . ."

This is what enticed me to go. Cat's last statement got my attention. Codie and I had been together for a year and we went everywhere together. I couldn't not go now.

"Fine," I sighed.

Cat squealed and threw a bandanna at me. The dark blue made me want to gag. I knew it resembled a horrible feud that had been going on for decades. I folded it and tucked it into my back pocket.

~*~

"Codie!" I felt like I was glowing as soon as I saw him. I ran and jumped into his arms, leaving Cat far behind me.

He clutched me close and whispered, "I didn't think you were coming."

"I had to. Cat wouldn't stop bugging me. Plus, you're here."

He set me down and kissed my forehead, a gesture that he knew I loved. It made me feel so comforted and it assured me that he wanted me, for me. "Stay in the back Mae. Hear me? The less people that come near you, the better. I don't want to have to explain to your sister why you have bruises." He chuckled and kissed my forehead again. This time, I just felt the sense of danger emanating from him. We both knew that this was a terrible place to be and neither of us wanted to have to be here. However, Codie's older brother was in charge of the gang, which obligated Codie to go and since I was with Codie, I had to go. Domino effect. So I let Codie crush me into his arms before I retreated to the edge of the park, where the least amount of people would see me.

~*~

Who was that? Why was he staring at me? I'm reminded of Codie, but Codie doesn't have blue eyes. Slowly, as I regained consciousness, I became aware of a pain in my abdomen. Oh God! It hurt! Why won't it stop? Was he hurting me? No, it's me. I can feel the short, smooth handle of a knife in my stomach. Don't cry Mae. Do not cry. However, I'm not as strong as I thought, and a single tear runs down my face. I took the moment to look at my surroundings and I realized that everyone had left. Even Codie. How could he? How could he abandon me while I die on the sidewalk? Anger spikes through me, but I'm grateful. That kid, with the stringy un-washed hair, dirty, worn-out clothes and sad, lonely eyes, that I didn't know had opened his heart to comfort a dying girl. His hand lightly stroked my hair, and I reached up to grab his arm. I tried to talk, but it came out as a whisper; he bent his head down to hear me.

"Thank-you." Simple words, but I could tell that he was relieved to hear them. He smiled down at me and continued running his fingers through my hair. It felt so nice, like when Codie holds me; it's comforting. I was getting so tired. My very eyelashes felt like weights. My body was so cold; it wasn't long before everything went black and my breath shuddered out.

CHAPTER ONE

It had been so long since I last saw the outside world. I shivered in my dark cell that I have called home for the past ten years as I waited for a guard to amble his way on by to let me out. Ten minutes passed before jingling keys alerted me to a guard's presence. I looked up with a small grin as he opened the door.

"What are you so happy about, Gorton?"

"Just nice to see you again Franc." He scowled at me before turning to lead me down the long hall of cells.

Looking at the concrete jungle around me, I was eager to get outside and see the world. I didn't actually do anything wrong; I was accused of a murder ten years ago. The girl that died, Mae, still haunted me in my dreams. Her vibrant green eyes leered out from the depths of my brain. I was pulled backwards in time as I walked.

She lay in a pool of her own blood, hands clenched around the wooden handle of a knife. Her eyes looked up at me, bravely but still pleading for help.

"Here you go."

"What?"

"Here you go, Gorton."

I shook my head, trying to focus on the present happenings. The portly secretary was looking at me impatiently, waiting for me to take the bundle from her hands. I grabbed it and looked through, finding a bit of pocket change and a cheque.

"Excuse me, what's this?" I inquired as I held up the cheque.

"It's a cheque, Mr. Gorton."

Thanks captain obvious.

"I got that, what's it for?"

"It's your inheritance, your mother passed away about a year ago."

While I was a little upset that I wasn't told about this, I wasn't really surprised. In fact, I was more surprised that there was money left for me to have. Nodding, I was escorted to a small change area and given a pair of street clothes. The pants handed to me were over-sized and were obviously meant for an obese person. The knees were worn and dirty and the back pockets were strained; Franc looked at me apologetically as I put them on. I stuffed the change and cheque into one of the front pockets and after pulling my pants up high began to exit the prison.

"Good luck Gorton, don't let me see you again."

I turned around and returned a small smile to Franc.

"I wouldn't give you the pleasure."

My first steps outside were glorious, like a caged bird being set free I whooped and took a moment to bask in the warm sun. I could still hear Franc laughing when I got in the cab. After watching the trees fly past and the prison building get smaller and smaller, I took the cheque out of my pocket. One hundred and fifty thousand dollars stared right at my face. I nearly choked. How in the world did she have that kind of money? Twelve years of heavy drinking should have used all of this up. Just as I was coming to the conclusion that this money must have been off-limits to her the cab stopped moving. In front of me sat a dingy hostel; I shoved the cheque back in my pocket and cautiously stepped out and away from the car.

The hostel door hung loosely on its hinges and shrieked in protest when I opened it. Previously white walls had turned grey with dirt and stale cigarette smoke that still hung heavily in the air. Furniture was shoved against walls; rejected, graffitied and unsalvageable. Dusty windows created an eerie glow throughout the room. I didn't want to stay here long; this place was even more disgusting than prison. The next morning, after washing in a mouldy shower I went into town to find somewhere else to live. The first thing I did, which seemed the most necessary, was open a bank account and receive a debit card.

After winding my way through the town, following the directions I was given at the bank, I found myself staring at a small business labeled "Homes 4 U." I stepped inside, breathing in the clean crisp air and was instantly happier. I walked up to the secretary, whose small rectangular glasses were perched precariously on the end of her nose, and waited for her to look up. When she did, her glasses slid and needed re-adjusting, her eyes crinkled at the corners due to her kind smile.

"What can I do for you?"

"I wanted to talk to a real estate agent please."

She nodded and after clicking some keys on the computer looked back up at me.

"You can go in the third office on the right."

I thanked her and eagerly strode down the hall. Waiting three doors to the right was the most beautiful woman I've ever seen. Her dark hair sat in a twisted bun on the top of her head, held in place by a bright pink pen. She beamed at me before introducing herself.

"Hello, I'm Ms. Siykes."

"Erik Gorton."

"Nice to meet you Erik, what can I do for you today?"

"I'm actually looking to rent an apartment."

"Okay."

She motioned for me to wait and strode out of the office. When she returned, a small red binder was clasped in her hands. She laid it on the desk in front of me and returned to her chair.

"How big of an apartment do you need?"

"Well, it's just me so a one room would be okay."

Her bright green eyes flashed, "Right at the front you'll find one rooms."

Flipping through the binder, there were three that I found in my price range and close to town.

"Can I see these ones?"

"Sure, we could go right now if that's okay with you."

"The sooner, the better."

She smiled at me and rose from her seat, a lock of hair falling into her face in the process. Her cheeks turned a slight shade of pink as she brushed it away, before leading me out of her office. While following her, I noticed how well her jacket hugged her waist.

"Janice, I'll be back in a bit."

The secretary, Janice, nodded and typed rapidly onto the computer before gazing in my direction. I glanced at her long enough to smile before following Olivia outside.

The first apartment we looked at was only a few minute walk away from the town centre. We entered the small grey room and automatically I knew that I didn't like it. It was too much like the apartment my mother and I had shared when I was younger. Everything was depressing and chipped, it even had peeling paint and water stains on the ceiling.

"Can we look at the next one? The pictures made this one look a lot better than it is."

"Yes, of course, no one really likes this one. It's been for sale for years."

"It just reminds me too much of my mother to be honest."

She smiled and let the subject drop, much to my relief. On our way to the second apartment we passed a quaint little restaurant that stuck in my mind. Its little curtained windows looked classy enough to not have screaming children and family photos on the inside. Two streets down from the restaurant was the second apartment; just across from a small park. It looked so happy with children laughing and playing that my spirits lifted.

"I like the looks of this one."

"You like children?"

"As long as they're not screaming I love them. They're so happy and free, it makes me want to re-live my childhood."

She giggled and looked at me, her eyes crinkled ever so slightly in the corners.

"Well, let's take a look shall we?"

She led me inside and opened the second door with a small silver key.

"Here we are."

I looked around at the beige walls of the main room and felt comforted. There was a small kitchen to my left that had two sky blue walls and dark wooden cabinets that matched the main door. The whole house was bare except for an old, sun-faded, worn chair that sat next to the large window in the living room area.

"I love it! I want to live here."

"Do you want to see the other one first?"

"No, thank-you though."

"Okay, we'll go back to my office and get you all set up then."

I moved into my apartment the next day, not that I actually had much to put in it. After closing the deal on my apartment the day before, I went to a furniture store. Picking out my furniture was the easy part; a black bed, couch, chair and a few tables. The worst part was getting it inside. The door to my apartment was just too small to fit the already assembled things through. I was forced to disassemble everything, bring it in and then put it back together. I even had to take that red chair out the same way; my hands turned red from washing them for so long. Luckily for me, my apartment was on the ground floor so I didn't have to drag that filthy thing too far. After I finished re-arranging my furniture the way I wanted it, I took a minute to relax in my new chair.

I sat on the faded green couch, arms wrapped around my knees. Looking at the grey walls around me, the absence of life screamed at me. The walls were devoid of pictures and instead, filled with dirt. My mother came home then, brown bag in hand.

"Mom, why don't we have any pictures?"

"GET TO BED! NOW!"

That was the first of many times that she came home screaming at me. I scampered to bed and laid there, listening to dishes slamming and my mother's sobbing growing gradually quieter until it stopped altogether. I cautiously stepped out of bed and tried to sneak around the corner of the doorway when jail cell bars slammed closed in my face. I screamed and begged, pleading to be let out and trying to persuade anyone that I didn't do it. Then it turned black.

Startled, I bolted awake and looked around at my surroundings. The loud slam was in fact, just the window next to me closing in the breeze. I shuffled to the bathroom and threw cold water on my face. I wiped most of the water off with my arm and examined myself in the mirror. Hard blue eyes stared back at me from beneath blonde hair that was in need of a trim.

The stark white clock on the wall told me it was almost three o'clock in the afternoon. On my way out of the apartment, my stomach rumbled, loudly. Food first, hair later.

A few blocks away, I found a large store that claimed to have everything. This was the perfect place to begin shopping and get some food. I stepped into the air conditioned doorway and went looking.

I left the store an hour later with an armful of bags. Struggling, I started my trek back home; I was almost halfway there when my shoe hit a crack in the sidewalk and I stumbled. Bags went tumbling to the ground; I swore and ducked down to retrieve the lost items. Just when I reached out to grab a shirt, a small hand grabbed it. Looking up I saw the radiant smile belonging to Ms. Siykes.

"I believe you dropped this."

I grinned, "Yeah, thank-you."

"Not a problem Erik. Do you want me to help?"

I nodded and handed her a few of the lightest bags before starting to plod home.

She looked up at me, "Are you from here? I've never seen you around before."

"I . . . left ten years ago and I just felt that it was time to come back. What about you?"

"I've been here my whole life. I can't leave."

"Or what?" I chuckled, "Will the monsters get you?"

"I wish. I'm just afraid of forgetting." She smiled, weakly.

"Forgetting what?"

"My sister."

"Oh." I looked down, awkwardly as we neared the apartment building. She pushed the lobby door open with her hip and held it for me.

Jokingly bowing to her I stated, "I guess chivalry is dead."

She laughed at me and danced inside before the door closed. "You can hold the next one."

I carefully laid down a handful of bags and dug through my pockets to find my key. After pulling it from my pocket, I unlocked the door and held it open. "After you."

She smiled brightly before stepping inside. "Wow, it looks so homey now!"

I smiled again; she seemed to have this effect on me. "Would you like a drink?"

"Do you have coffee?"

"I can try to make some." I started looking through the bags for coffee supplies and pulling everything out of the doorway at the same time.

"I don't want to be troublesome, let me help." She started emptying bags and putting their contents into the correct rooms before I could even protest. I shook my head silently and began following the instructions on the coffee can carefully. Before too long, the smell of coffee was thick in the air and all my purchases were put away. While I poured two mugs of coffee Ms. Siykes stood by the kitchen table, watching me.

"What do you do for a living?"

"Nothing right now. I was going to go job hunting tomorrow."

"Well, I know this place that's hiring; I'm friends with the owner. If you tell her I sent you, I'm sure she'll hire you."

"Wow, you're my guardian angel Ms. Siykes!"

"Call me Olivia."

"Okay Olivia, how much sugar do you want?"

CHAPTER TWO

It was too late after Olivia left for me to do anything of interest, so I jumped into bed and fell asleep. If you could call it sleep anyways-I tossed and turned all night. Every noise my apartment made turned into jail cells slamming and bodies falling. Needless to explain, I woke up wide-eyed and tangled in my bedding. To add to the already great morning, I didn't know that I had been tangled and proceeded to fall on my face when I stood up.

"Damnit!" I growled and kicked furiously at the blankets to free myself before going to take a shower.

Half an hour later, when I had used all the hot water, I retreated from the shower and sat at my kitchen table with a cup of coffee. According to the clock Olivia had placed in the middle of my table, it was just getting to be seven o'clock. Sighing, I threw on a white V-neck, downed the rest of my coffee, slipped on some shoes and headed out to explore. I quickly found the restaurant Olivia had mentioned-Horizons-and continued around the block to waste some time. The corner building was a small gym that looked like it hadn't seen a living person in at least ten years and just beyond that was a little barber shop. This whole part of town seemed so old-fashioned, and I loved it immediately.

Flickering lights in the barber shop beckoned at me until I sauntered inside, determined to do something about the mop on my head before going to an interview. What met me inside was a wiry man with only a few grey hairs left on his head. Gold rimmed glasses pressed against his eyebrows, which was apparently where all the hair from his head had gone, when he smiled at me.

"What can I do for you sir?"

"Just a haircut, if you don't mind."

"Of course, I'll just get my daughter. I'm much too shaky at this age."

I smirked, relieved when he disappeared into the back of the room. That smirk however, turned into a slight grimace when the man's daughter returned in his place. A tall, lanky, blonde strutted around the corner with her red bra-which hardly contained her extra-large breasts-strikingly visible through her white blouse. She smiled seductively at me with lips as red as her bra and beckoned me towards a chair.

"What can I do for you today?"

"U-uhm, just a haircut, thanks."

Her round, full lips turned to a pout, "that's all?"

I cleared my throat and tried to focus on the wall, "Yes please. I'm not sure what to do with it, just make it look good."

Her smile returned and stayed plastered on her face throughout the haircut. She didn't even flinch when her chest pressed into the back of my head. I on the other hand, turned bright red and focused even harder on the wall.

Afterwards, I paid and left quickly, desperately wanting out of her reach before she dragged me to her house. In my hurry, I ran into a larger woman in a light purple track suit.

"Oh my gosh, I'm sorry!"

"Oh, hush now dearie. I know my behind's large, it was partially mah fault." A southern accent altered the words and made the woman seem almost comical.

I watched her sidle up to a dark, wooden door and unlock it. A quick look up reminded me that this was the restaurant that I was going to for an interview.

"Excuse me? Are you the manager?"

"Why yes dearie, I am. Are ya lookin' for me?"

I nodded, "Yes ma'am, I'm Erik Gorton. I have an interview."

"Ah! Yes, I remember. Come on in Erik, I'm Ms. Ayna."

~*~

When I left Ms. Ayna's office I wasn't sure I'd be getting a job. I had no experience and not many people wanted a released felon around them. However, she seemed to understand when I explained my side of the story to her and she had a ball teasing me after I told her not to relay this information to Olivia. She even went so far as to sing about it, which sent me into another fit of blushing.

On my way home I studied the building around me, noting which of them looked shady and where all the places to eat were. Something that really caught my eye was a bright orange building with signs strewn throughout the windows. They exclaimed that the restaurant was open twenty-four hours, while others claimed they had the best breakfast and dancing at night. I was greatly pleased that this bright little restaurant was only a couple minutes from my apartment.

Back in my apartment, I had sat on my couch to relax and ended up falling asleep. I awoke, hours later, to my phone ringing. Running to my kitchen, I skidded into the wall that the phone was mounted on and answered the phone groaning, "Hello?"

"Mr. Gorton?"

"Yes?"

"Hi, this is Ms. Ayna, I'm sorry to tell you . . . ."-I sighed, waiting for the rejection-"that you will now be working for me!"

I smiled broadly, "Thank-you! When do you want me to start?"

"Tomorrow morning at eight."

"Sounds good, see you tomorrow Ms. Ayna!"

I heard her chuckle, as I hung up the phone and danced my way to my room.

~*~

The next morning I woke up, startled out of a nightmare. Instead of the usual re-living of Mae's death, I saw Olivia die this time. Her bright green eyes glared up at me as if accusing me, saying that I could've helped.

Her eyes still had me shaken after my shower and coffee, so I phoned her. She answered after the fifth ring.

"Hello?" Her usual light voice was groggy with sleep, I chuckled.

"Morning sunshine."

"Erik, do you realize what time it is?"

"Six thirty, on the dot."

She sighed, "what do you want?"

"I just wanted to hear your lovely voice."

I could hear in her voice that she was smiling, "Attached already?"

We laughed together before I questioned, "Would you like to get coffee now that you're awake?"

"Erik. Nothing's open at this time!"

"I know a place, just come over."

"Is it your house? You can't make coffee, remember?"

I smirked, "No, I know a real place."

"Ten minutes."

The phone hung up, leaving a dial tone in my ear I smiled and lounged on my couch, waiting and watching outside my window. People were beginning their trips to work, getting early morning coffee, and going for runs. People watching was definitely my favourite hobby, with so much going on in a person's mind, and you can tell by their posture. That girl, going for a run in a sweater, kept her eyes down because she's self-conscious. That man, whose shoulders are stiff under his suit jacket, he's in desperate need of coffee and a job he wants to wake up for. Immersed in my thoughts I didn't hear knocking on the door until it became louder and more persistent. I bounded to the door and whisked it open, catching Olivia, who looked as good as ever, in mid-knock.

"Hello beautiful."

She smiled, "What was so urgent that you needed to wake me up at six thirty?"

I shoved my feet into a pair of sneakers, "I'll explain on the way. Let's go."

I stayed quiet most of the way to the cafe until Olivia looked up at me and demanded, "Well, are you going to tell me or what?"

"Persistent. Well, basically, I just had a nightmare that you were murdered and you were mad at me because I couldn't help you."

Her eyes twinkled. "Glad to know you worry about me."

I smiled nervously, "Yeah, just worried."

"So, do you know where you're going? Everything looks closed."

"Just wait. It's around this corner."

Her eyebrow rose in disbelief but she followed me around the corner to the entrance of the orange building.

"Here we are."

"I've never seen this place before, are you sure?"

"Nope."

"What?" I grabbed her before she changed her mind and yanked her forward through the doors. We arrived out of breath and receiving odd looks from the people within. Olivia, who was now completely awake, pulled me across the room to a small booth. Almost instantly after we sat down a girl with dying, cropped, rust coloured hair and piercings covering most of her face appeared.

She batted her heavily lined eyes at me, "My name is Nikki, and I'm going to be your server this morning. What can I get for you?"

Olivia examined the table menu for a minute, "I'll have a coffee and a carrot muffin."

Nikki forced a smile on her pudgy face, "Excellent. For you sir?"

"The same please, but I would also like bacon and eggs. Scrambled."

She batted her eyes again and twitched away, large hips swaying back and forth. As soon as she was out of range, Olivia and I burst out laughing.

"She wants you. Did you see that?"

"Scared of a little competition Olivia?"

"You're joking right?" At my serious gaze she started speaking faster, more urgently, "she's disgusting! She smells bad too."

"Maybe she thinks you're disgusting."

She looked at me in disbelief, "I think you're demented."

Faking hurt I grabbed her hand and looked in her eyes, "Do you really wish that pain upon my soul? Am I not good enough to deserve the great Olivia Siykes?"

She giggled, "You're incredibly ridiculous Erik."

"You called me incredible!" I beamed.

"Incredibly *ridiculous*," she laughed and shook her head at me.

"Well, if I wasn't then we wouldn't be having this much fun."

"This is true." Her cute smile was all I could look at until Nikki waddled up with our food.

"Two muffins, coffee, and eggs and bacon for the man." Again with the batting eyes. It definitely wasn't enough to make me see past her metal face, dead hair, caked on make-up and candy dust around her mouth.

"Thank-you Nikki, you're amazing." I winked at her just to make Olivia ogle and dug into my food before Nikki twitched away, tossing her hair.

Olivia's jaw drooped so low I was afraid it might fall off, "Close your mouth. Someone will think there's something wrong with you and wonder why I took you out in public."

She snapped her mouth closed at frowned at me, "You're such a flirt!"

Picking off a piece of muffin, I smiled at her, "Jealous? I didn't think you'd be so attached already."

Olivia scowled and slurped at her coffee, "You're unbelievable."

"Thank-you."

~*~

I left Olivia at seven-thirty and took my time walking to work. I didn't have to be in until eight, so I had plenty of time to drift off and think about Olivia. We weren't moving fast but I knew I was falling as quickly as a bag of bricks from a plane. Soon enough, I'd hit the ground hard and stay there. In my heart I knew I had met Olivia for a reason, why else did my heart pound like a beating drum whenever I saw her? There was just one thing-before I met her I hardly had nightmares and now for some reason I was having them every night. She looked nothing like Mae, so why did I keep substituting them?

"Erik! You're just in time!" Ms. Ayna called from the other side of the street. She beckoned me inside with an arm encased in tight orange material. I bounded up the steps quickly and followed her inside. While listening to Ms. Ayna explain what I'd be doing I took a moment to look around. Dark blue walls gave a stark contrast against light wood flooring. Dozens of glossy black tables with blue napkins and mats pulled the whole thing together.

"So, because of your . . . history, your shifts will start light. You'll work the morning for a few days to see if you like working here and then, if you decide to stay, you can work the lunch as well."

I bit back my protests and nodded silently.

"Great! Your uniform is in the back."

"Awesome." I stalked to the back of the restaurant and into a staff room. Inside was a couch, table and a large closet stuffed with clothing. Each person had a hanger, with their name on it, which their uniform and street clothes hung on. All the men's uniforms were the same black pants and shirt with a blue tie. I wonder what Ms. Ayna's favourite color was.

I changed quickly into the uniform but got stuck trying to do up the tie. I had no clue where to start; tie tying isn't something you're taught in prison. Frustrated, I exited the staff room with the wrinkled tie hung around my neck.

"I can't do this!"

Ms. Ayna stood in front of me, trying to hold back her laughter, "Need help, dearie?"

"Please."

Her chubby fingers were unusually long and nimble, I gawked at her when she had the tie done up in a matter of seconds.

She smiled, "Piano. You ready?"

"As I'll ever be."

"Good." She handed me a small notepad to write orders on and sidled away as I strode out to greet customers.

~*~

When my shift ended I smelled like sweat and food, which was quite disgusting. Waiting on people was nothing like working out. Waiting on people requires mental abilities, not just how much you can bench press. I dropped more than one plate, on myself, and brought some food to the wrong tables. The one thing I was thankful for was patient people; all the people seated in my section were kind and didn't pester me about not knowing what I was doing. After thanking Ms. Ayna for letting me work I raced home and took another shower. I can't stand being dirty.

I was just getting out of the shower when I heard knocking on the door. Swearing, I threw a pair of boxers on and ran to answer the door. Waiting for me was Olivia, who blushed when she saw my unclothed body.

"U-uhm . . . I'll just . . . uh," she bit her lip nervously. "Do you want to put clothes on?"

"I was about to when you came knocking."

She grinned and followed me inside, stopping to sit in a chair while I retreated to my room. While hurriedly throwing on pants, I shook stray water from my hair.

"I just wanted to know if you wanted to come to lunch with me if you're not busy."

"You're kidding right? You're the only person I know besides Ms. Ayna."

"Well there's Nikki . . ."

I pulled a black t-shirt over my head and returned to the living room, looking at her, "No need to be so insecure Olivia. Besides, I don't feel like having my pelvis crushed."

She giggled and looked at my outfit, "Nice belt."

Looking down, I saw the handcuff buckle and grinned, "You have no idea. Why are you looking there anyways? Weirdo."

Olivia's face flushed red as she stammered, "Well . . . Uhhmm . . . . I . . . ."

Laughing, I laid my hand on her shoulder, "Calm down, I'm just kidding. Where are we going?"

"Surprise."

The surprise turned out to be a picnic next to a lake. Olivia set up a blanket underneath a pale pink tree and started unpacking as I looked around. The lake's water was a brilliant blue that shone in the sun. There was a serene silence in the air, which was suspected on a Monday at one in the afternoon. I eventually sat with Olivia under the tree and began munching on small sandwiches. A small pink flower rained down from the tree and landed in my lap. I looked at it for a moment before reaching over and tucking it behind Olivia's ear. She looked down and blushed before putting her face close to mine. I felt her nose graze my cheek just before I heard, "Wanna go swimming?"

I looked up into Olivia's smiling face before she raced off, peeling her bright yellow dress off to reveal a black and red bikini. Running after her, I jumped out of my shoes and pants and finally rid myself of my shirt. I watched her dive smoothly into the water and come back up looking at me.

"Get in here already!"

I splashed through the water and slipped under the surface quickly before resurfacing, sputtering, "That's freezing!"

"I know," Olivia giggled and splashed at me.

I sunk beneath the water and swam forward until my arms were wrapped around Olivia's slender legs. Pulling down hard, I heard her shriek before falling into the water. I pushed her shoulders down and propelled myself upward, breaking the surface loudly. It wasn't long before I saw Olivia surface with a look of anger on her face.

"You jerk! What if I couldn't swim?"

I chuckled, "Then you wouldn't suggest swimming, Olivia."

She smirked, "You're quick, Erik Gorton. Too quick."

CHAPTER THREE

I'd know Olivia for 6 short weeks. We'd helped each other grow more than two people normally would. The only explanation I could think of to explain was that we loved each other; I knew deep down that I loved her like none other before. However, I wasn't positive of her love for me; I was sure that it was there but we'd failed to communicate it to each other. I do know that there must be a reason we saw each other at least once a day, due partially to the fact that Olivia was a regular at the Horizons restaurant. She'd introduced me to her parents there who, due to their accent, called me "Ereek". I didn't pay much attention to them and their French banter after they told me all about how they lived in France and left to learn the English language so their children would have no language boundaries. Olivia and her sister were brought up learning two languages and spoke them both fluently. Her sister was the information I pushed for the most, I wanted to know everything. However, it was like the subject had been locked behind bars. From what I saw of their house, there were only blank spaces where pictures used to be. In my opinion it was because pictures meant explaining and explaining was too painful for them. However, for all my prying I still couldn't get any information. Olivia eventually told me that if I stopped asking about her sister, then she wouldn't ask about my childhood. I eagerly complied.

No matter how much being with Olivia comforted me, she couldn't save me from my nightmares. What used to be just vivid flashbacks were now tainted. They featured Olivia now and skipped between the murder, jail cells and just blackness. However, the same screaming was heard in every scene like background music. The same screaming I heard 10 years ago from a crowd of people who thought they could outrun what they let happen. More than once a week I woke up shaking and breathing as if I had run a marathon. I took to perching in my bedroom window, watching early morning drivers disappear down the road and admiring the sunrise. I felt somewhat like Quasimodo from The Hunchback of Notre Dame, just watching the world around them and being in a completely different world of your own. A world where you could sit and let your past and problems haunt you without people on the outside knowing. Or you could escape and imagine yourself living a perfect life, with joy and light, where no one would judge you based on what you've done. I never understood people's need to have alone time until now; their only want being time to think or dream until the real world needed them to come back. When I finished "brooding" as Olivia calls it, I usually phoned her. We'd started to go on coffee dates every morning, since I'm awake so early and tend to wake her up before her alarm even thinks about going off. Fortunately, she never sounded angry. She was getting a little bit worried about my constant nightmares though, suggesting that I talk to someone, but I shrugged it off and hurriedly changed the subject. I tried to keep a fun, light air with Olivia, knowing that underneath that professional look was a girl who was still traumatized over her sister. Being as such, I often asked if she had heard new rumours about us; we were apparently a popular couple. The mysterious guy who showed up out of nowhere and the girl who wanted to get everything all on her own. Olivia didn't even look twice at most men, knowing that she didn't need someone to take after her in any way. She'd survived ten years and everybody knew she could survive a hundred more; so why was she with me? I was told that it was because of my good looks.

Knocking at the door pulled me from my thoughts and sent me hurrying towards the door. Once there I paused to run a hand through my hair, messing it enough to look like I hadn't a care in the world about my appearance. Upon opening it I grinned and closed my eyes, awaiting the usual fling-me-backwards-hug. However, it was not a hug I received; a pair of lips hungrily pressed against mine, pushing me back a step in the process. I pushed back, pressing our bodies together to the point where we could have been one in the same. When my hands fell down to caress a pair of large, chunky hips instead of slender, boney ones, I knew it wasn't Olivia. Startled, I reeled backwards to find two women staring at me. Nikki, whose already large body was even more defined in a short skirt and tight, red tank top, stared at me as if my reaction confused her. Standing beside her was Olivia, whose eyes showed a girl who could kill without a second thought. *If looks could kill.* Olivia turned and began to storm away when I pushed Nikki out of my way.

"Olivia, wait! She kissed me, I thought it was you!"

She turned then, glaring at me, "You thought I was THAT?!"

I shook my head, "My eyes were closed, but after I-"

"Leave me alone Erik!" She interrupted and stalked away, leaving me looking like a jerk in the hallway.

While retreating to my apartment, I took a moment to look at Nikki. She looked like a lost child, who was in desperate need of a bath.

I heard a noise like a whimper before she asked, "What'd she mean by 'THAT'?"

"It means you're fat and ugly; now get out of my sight before I slam your head in this door." My words were clipped with anger; I could decapitate her, if it wouldn't send me back to prison of course. Instead, I watched her hulking shape disappear out of the hallway and onto the street. By the time she was gone I had yanked my bag off the table and was slamming the door behind me. I took the long way, walking down and around two blocks, to the gym to try and walk off some rage but I was still furious when the sky became dark and I turned down the street to the gym. In this state of mind I didn't notice Olivia until she had run past me. Olivia never ran; what was going on? It was only moments before I got my answer. A big, burly guy came running after her, spitting curses. She must not have seen me because she screeched for help, sending my mind to another time. I watched again as Mae was stabbed before my eyes. Only, my memory was cut short by that guy pushing past me violently. I wasn't going to be too late this time.

I chased after him, grabbing the back of his shirt and pulling him off course. He whirled and narrowed his bloodshot eyes at me while a growl emanated from his chest.

"THIS IS NONE OF YOUR BUSINESS!"

"Well, actually it is. You did push me after all and that is my girfriend you're chasing. Therefore, it's my business." Complete lie, Olivia and I weren't dating. However, he didn't need to know that.

That was the end of our nice conversation though. He charged at me, throwing a punch to my jaw and causing me to stumble back a few steps. I paused for a second and retaliated with a hit to his eye. We both fell to the ground when he jumped at me and unfortunately I landed underneath him. It took him no time at all to recover and start beating on my face. I tasted blood and then the next thing I knew, I had rolled over and was now hitting this guy repeatedly while he tried to defend himself. Suddenly, I felt something crunch under my hand and I stopped. Looking at his face I saw that his eye had swollen and turned black and his nose was gushing blood. I scrambled off him and crouched near my gym bag, watching him rise to his feet.

"You'll regret this, pretty boy."

I was watching him stalk away when a slender hand lay on my shoulder, causing me to jump. Olivia stepped back a couple steps when I whirled around and waited to see if I'd hit her.

Once I had relaxed she smiled and said, "I didn't mean to frighten you, I just wanted to thank you."

Her glassy green eyes glimmered with tears, and I stared at them. There was something eerily familiar about her . . . . Her eyes! They were the same as Mae's! A million questions raced through my mind but I suppressed them and stepped forward to embrace Olivia. Her small body shivered with the cold and her fear and I clutched her tighter.

"Ssshh, its okay Olivia. You're okay."

"That was my ex-boyfriend. I tried to get a restraining order . . . He scares me, Erik." She nestled her head into the crook of my shoulder and tried to calm her breathing.

"I know, its okay. I'll protect you as long as you stay with me."

She sniffed and looked up into my eyes, "Are you sure?"

"As long as you want me here."

"I'll always want you here."

CHAPTER FOUR – OLIVIA

I watched Erik's lean body as he worked out. Everything looked so effortless when he moved. Muscles I didn't know existed rippled in the dim lights. I was definitely mesmerized. However, I was still confused by Erik's quick change of mood. After the mishap with Taylor, Erik was comforting and loving. Once we got in vicinity of the gym though, his blue eyes started darkening and his mouth set in a tight line. He stopped talking, and I was left alone with my thoughts. Which made me realize that Erik had called me his girlfriend. I mean, I know we're inseparable but I'd never considered us together. He did fight for me though, which only strengthened the love I had begun to feel for him. I shivered and wrapped myself tighter in Erik's tight black sweater. It seemed like everything he owned was black, but in Erik's defense, it was a great color on him. It made his blonde hair brighten and gave him a bad-boy look. This effect was completed by his lack of past; well, past he'd tell my anyways. It was as though he had just appeared out of the blue.

"She was a drunk."

I looked up to find icy blue eyes staring at me, "Pardon me?"

"My mother. When I was seven, my dad died and she became an alcoholic. She died a couple years ago."

I rose to my feet and wrapped my arms around his stiff shoulders. Erik hesitated before relaxing and enveloping me in his arms.

"My sister was murdered." With Erik's head buried in my hair, I heard his breath catch but I ignored it.

"I'm . . . I'm so sorry . . . when?"

"We were fifteen. She snuck out one night and never came back. The police found a boy with her body and threw him in jail. They told us he was homeless . . . Probably just wanted money." My shoulders sagged when tears started to pour from my eyes. What is it about him that makes me want to bare my soul to him? His hand made small, soothing circles on my back, and I sniffed.

"Sorry, this is a lot to tell you."

"Don't be sorry, we were bound to tell each other sooner or later."

My words kept flowing like a waterfall, "I used to stay up wishing they had executed that boy, but when I saw him on TV he looked so helpless and sad. I was ready to smash the screen, and then he showed up, pleading not guilty and looking like a beaten puppy. Then, I wasn't mad anymore. I just wanted to comfort him. Especially because he was all alone and I was feeling the same way."

"Do you . . . remember him?"

"Not very well. It's been so long. I just remember his hair. It was such a light blonde." Erik let go of me and stripped off his shirt, causing me to blush. "What are you doing?"

He looked at me and smirked, "My shirt was getting cold." I passed him his bag and he immediately began rummaging through it and exchanged his sweaty shirt for a clean blue one.

"You own something that isn't black?"

He looked at me curiously before he started laughing. "Of course I do. Don't be ridiculous!"

My smile broadened when Erik wrapped an arm around my waist. Then I remembered, "So, apparently I'm your girlfriend now?"

He hesitated a moment before answering, "I thought it was the right thing to say at the time. Plus, we might as well be."

"I don't remember agreeing to that."

He stopped walking and turned me so that we were facing each other. "Olivia, will you please be my girlfriend?"

I blushed, feeling millions of butterflies in my stomach. It took me a second but I finally choked out, "Of course I will, Erik."

Erik's reaction was immediate; he pulled me into his arms and squeezed me tight. I was crushed against his chest but I wouldn't have moved for the life of me. I felt like everything was right in the world, and then he kissed me. I could feel my heart explode in my chest; it was everything I could have imagined. It perfectly explained a growing love, starting out hesitant but blossoming into something wonderful. We pulled away from each other and laced our fingers together. Walking back to Erik's, we never said a word. We had no need to-our smiled said enough for us. We still had smiles on our faces when we fell asleep clutching each other tightly.

CHAPTER FIVE

I was trapped in a dimly lit room. There was a thin layer of frost that refused to melt, covering the walls. I turned in a circle and found a small window mocking me from far away. The closer I got, the farther away it moved. I was reduced to yelling and pleading, my teenage hands clenched at my sides.

"Erik!"

I cried out, "Please! I didn't do it! I swear!"

My body started shaking violently, the small voice getting increasingly more desperate in its attempts to gain my attention.

"Erik! Wake up, please!"

I gasped loudly, eyes snapping open. There was a woman peering down at me worriedly, her dark hair wild with sleep. Her small, smooth hand stroked my cheek lovingly.

"What didn't you do, Erik?"

I scrunched my eyes shut and swore, "You heard?"

The corner of her lip slid up into a half-smile and it was then that I remembered. This girl was Olivia, my girlfriend of the past two months. We were lying in the master bedroom of her house and I had just had my first nightmare in weeks.

"It's hard not to hear when you're yelling. Now, what didn't you do?"

I sighed, exhausted and looked into her sparkling green eyes, "I can't... I can't tell you, Olivia."

Her eyebrows pinched together, the way they always did when she got upset. "Why can't you? You tell me everything else! Erik, I know almost everything about you from your favourite color to everything about your mother. The only thing I don't know is the base of your dreams! Please, just tell-"

"Nightmares," I interrupted while pressing the heels of my hands into my eyes.

"What?"

"Dreams are good, these are *not*."

She rolled her eyes, huffing loudly. The bed shifted as she got up and walked away. Groaning, I got up and followed her.

"Olivia. Please, I really can't tell you."

She whirled around, eyes brimming with hateful tears. "Why can't you? Do you not trust me?"

I gawked, "Olivia, I trust you with my whole life! I just don't trust my past."

A small tear escaped her eye, which I promptly wiped off with my thumb. She turned her face into my hand, nuzzling it. I wrapped my other arm around her waist and pulled us together. Olivia's hands clutched at my back, holding me tightly. I bent my head down to kiss Olivia's forehead and spent a moment inhaling the smell of her hair. Her whole body shuddered against me with a shaky exhale.

"I love you, Erik."

"I love you, Olivia."

She looked up at me, eyes gleaming and lightly pressed her lips against mine. I smiled and buried my head in her hair. We stayed like that, un-moving, for what seemed like an eternity until the doorbell rang.

CHAPTER SIX

What stood in the doorway almost gave me a heart attack. Two men in dark suits stared at me with Taylor, Olivia's ex, smirking between them. The men pulled leather pouches from their pockets and flashed shiny ID badges at me in one smooth, practiced motion.

"Detective Morillo; this is my partner Detective Ennen. Are you Erik Gorton?"

Olivia side-stepped behind me, clenching my hand tightly.

"If this is about his broken nose, I'm sorry. He was intimidating Olivia and attacked me when I confronted him. It was self-defense."

"Mr. Gorton, this is more serious than your tussle with Mr. Guyon." Detective Ennen leered up at me, his flat face scrunched up. "May we come in?"

I could tell by the angry flash in their eyes that Olivia had looked at them and shook her head. "I'm sorry. He's not allowed on my property."

Detective Morillo's bushy eyebrows knitted together, "Well the, we'll just have to come back with a warrant."

They turned and walked away from us, leaving Taylor hesitating a moment to glare at me before following. I closed the door slowly before whirling around and hiding my face within my hands. "Oh my god! Shit! Damnit!" I yelled curses into my hands, knowing but not caring anymore that Olivia was bound to find out about what happened to me.

Her gentle hands grasped mine and tried to pull them away from my face, "Erik, what happened?"

I shook my head, "I don't know! I haven't broken probation or anything! What the hell do they want?"

Her hands twitched, "Probation? Erik, tell me what happened. Right now!"

I moved my hands to look at her, "I was in prison."

Her hands dropped as her face took on a look of pure horror, "What?"

I sighed, "I was accused of murder ten and a half years ago. In the park. I was there when a girl died and I was thrown in jail."

Her hand fluttered near her mouth, "Mae . . . The white haired boy . . ."

I nodded solemnly. "Me."

Olivia's knees buckled, sending her sliding to the floor. She sat there, whimpering, "no," like a mantra. She didn't want to believe it, but she did.

I crouched down next to her, "Please Olivia, you know that I didn't do it." I reached out to grab her hand, but she flinched away from me and muttered something incoherent. "What did you say?"

"MURDERER!" Her voice cracked, but her eyes were cold and harsh; I withdrew my arm. "GET OUT OF MY HOUSE!"

Rising to my feet, I sighed and left through the doorway to retrieve my belongings from Olivia's room. I wasn't surprised to see she hadn't moved when I returned. I grabbed the door handle and twisted it. I turned back before I left and stared at Olivia for a second, "I love you." I murmured, and then I left.

CHAPTER SEVEN – OLIVIA

"That bastard!" I screeched, slapping my hands against the floor. Jumping to my feet, I scrambled around to look for signs of Erik in my living room. The glint of a small silver frame caught my eye. Frozen on the paper inside was a shot of Erik and I, sitting in his apartment. His eyes showed no signs of the dark clouds that crossed them when he was upset. Instead, they were clear and bright like concentrated pieces of sky. He had his nose buried into my dark curls, breathing in the vanilla scented shampoo he loved so much. I looked so content and ready to face whatever challenges came at me, as long as I could be with him. Running my thumb over the picture, I began to cry. Tears fell from my face and onto the glass of the frame. Clutching the picture to my chest, I slumped to the floor and continued to cry until the world went dark.

~*~

I drifted in and out of sleep for three days, only awakening to pick the picture back up. This time I stayed awake long enough to see that my answering machine was blinking with messages; I wouldn't be surprised if they were all from Erik. I didn't want to hear what he said though, there was nothing else to explain. He went to jail for the murder of my sister; there was no one else there, so if he didn't kill her, who did? I dragged myself to the bathroom and threw up before falling back asleep.

"Olivia, answer your phone, please. I swear . . ."

"Olivia. You haven't shown up to work for a week! If this continues . . ."

Knock knock

I groaned and lifted my head off the tiled floor, peering out through heavy eyelids.

"Olivia?"

I crawled out of the bathroom and collapsed back on the ground. No one should have to see me like this. A key turned in the door, allowing access to whoever was at the door. The sharp clicks of a stiletto shoe told me that a woman had entered.

"Olivia honey, it's time to get up."

"Why didn't I move the key?" I groaned.

Cat giggled and stood over me, looking as sexy as always in tight black jeans and a matching leather jacket. Cat, whose real name was Kathy, had been my friend since elementary school. She pulled me out of my slump when Mae died and I did the same for her when her father murdered her mother. She even lived with me for a couple years, seeing as she was still a minor when they died. Apparently, it was her turn to save me again. She laid a pink bag on the floor behind her and bent down to scoop me up in her arms. You wouldn't tell by looking at her, but Cat was all muscle and worked hard to keep herself that way. Effortlessly, she carried me to the couch and laid me down with my head in her lap.

"Olivia, this is getting silly. People are starting to think you died, and I can tell that you haven't moved from the floor in days."

"How?"

She grinned down at me, "You stink."

I rolled my eyes, "I hate you."

Cat sighed and lifted me up again, carrying me to the bathroom. She set me down next to the shower and turned it on, "You have twenty minutes. Get in."

She left and I could immediately hear her talking to herself while she moved around my kitchen. I huffed and peeled off my sweaty clothes before I stepped into the steaming water.

I exited the shower and wrapped myself in a towel before shuffling to my room. Cat was sitting on my bed impatiently tapping her nails against her leg.

Her face lit up when she saw me, "Improvement! I've got Chinese food coming, tea is made, and I brought movies; now get dressed."

CHAPTER EIGHT

I spent three days trying to contact Olivia, only to listen to a recording of her voice. I knew she was there because nobody had seen her since. I sat at home for two more days, waiting for her to answer, until Detective Morillo and Detective Ennen stopped by. They even had a warrant in case I was going to be stubborn, but I had learned my lesson years ago. In order to make it through alive, you had to do as told. Any and all stupidity would be punished.

Detective Morillo cleared his throat with an unnecessarily loud cough, "Mr. Gorton. May we come inside?"

I nodded and led the two men into my living room, gesturing for them to have a seat. They sat on the couch and leaned forward, watching me while I settled into my chair.

"Did you know an Antonio Seiberling, Mr. Gorton?"

"No sir, I did not."

"Are you absolutely sure?" Detective Ennen peered up at me as if I had sprouted a second head.

I sighed, "Yes sir, I'm positive. Why do you ask?"

He poured the contents of a pouch onto the table between us, spilling pictures of a dead man between us. The skin around his lips had taken on a blue hue and there was a single knife wound in his stomach. My stomach lurched and I turned away to stare at the carpet.

Detective Morillo watched me and launched right into an explanation. "Antonio Seiberling was found dead a week ago. The knife used to kill him was the same model used to kill Mae Siykes."

"So what, you think I'm a serial killer now? I don't understand, why come to me?"

Detective Ennen was the first to break the silence that followed my question. "Did you kill Mr. Seiberling?"

Rolling my eyes, I huffed out an answer, "No sir, I did not kill Antonio. Take DNA and lie detector tests if you really want to."

Detective Morillo smirked, "Oh, we will. Don't you worry." After reaching into his coat pocket, he retrieved a long cotton swab in a plastic tube. "Open." I let my jaw hang open and looked up at him with a tired look. He quickly swirled the swab against my cheek and dropped it back into the tube. "Thank you, Mr. Gorton. We'll keep in touch."

Then they left, taking all evidence that they had been here with them. I stared at the table for a while before lying on the couch and falling asleep.

*

I was lounging around my house the next morning when there was a knock on my door. I glanced over at the door and yelled. "It's open!" It didn't surprise me when the two detectives plodded over the threshold.

"Mr. Gorton, our chief would appreciate if you could accompany us downtown."

Looking down at my naked chest, I raised an eyebrow, "Can I get dressed?"

The detectives smiled and nodded, which allowed me to go to my room where my thoughts went wild. A million questions started running around my brain; What is Olivia doing? Is she okay? Am I going back to jail? Where would that leave her? Should I confess? Will they even believe me? I dug a small box out from under my bed and was just putting the final touches on a letter when my phone rang.

"Hello?"

"Well hello there daddy."

"Kathy, that's a bit sexual for people who've just met."

"It's Cat! And you're going to be a father!"

"This is terrible timing Cat! I'm going down to the police station soon!"

"Sorry!" Her giggling echoed in my ear even after she hung up the phone. I swore and hastily added another sentence to the letter and shoved it back under my bed. I returned to my living room, fully clothed, and looked straight at the detectives.

"I'd like to give a statement."

Detective Ennen's eyebrows raised in question, "Oh? What about?"

"I'd like to share the truth about Mae's death." Detective Morillo's shoulders visibly tensed before he reached into his briefcase to extract a recorder and another small electronic device. "What's that?"

"It's a smaller version of a lie detector. Generally, it's used if our cars aren't working but I think it will be easier for you to tell us here rather than at the station." Immediately, he began untangling wires and attaching them to my fingers.

Detective Ennen set the recorder in front of me and clicked the record button, "This is Detective Ennen and Detective Morillo receiving a statement on this August 13th about the Mae Siykes case and relating to the Antonio Seiberling case from one Erik Gorton. This is related, correct, Mr. Gorton?"

"Yes sir."

"And you are giving this statement out of your own free will, correct?"

"Yes sir."

"Good. Begin when you're ready."

I took a shaky breath and exhaled loudly, "I would like to start off by saying that I did not kill Mae Siykes. However, I was present during her final moments. I was a fifteen year old boy living on the streets and curious about the sounds I heard in the park. What I found was a gang fight. Mae was at the back of the crowd, obviously uncomfortable, looking into the distance. A boy who, for the record, looked a lot like Antonio Seiberling ran up to her and stabbed her. Just as quickly as he had stabbed her, he ran away. Him and everyone else, they all turned and ran away; everyone, except me. Instead of running away, I ran towards her. I'm not sure why, but I just felt that I should. I consoled her until she passed; right after she passed, I was arrested. I spent 10 years in jail and now, here I am."

Detective Morillo blinked a few times and cleared his throat, "Just for the record, did you kill Antonio Seiberling out of revenge?"

I sighed, "No, sir. I did not kill Antonio Seiberling. In my opinion, the guilt started to eat away at him and he offed himself."

"Thank you."

The devices were shut off and put away in silence. Detective Ennen was the first to talk, "You realize that you'll still need to come with us, correct?"

I nodded, "Of course. I just need to clear up that if I'm sent back to prison, I want everything to be given to Olivia Siykes."

They nodded in unison, "Yes sir."

CHAPTER NINE – OLIVIA

"Cat! Oh god, wake up!" I clutched my stomach and shook her until her eyes snapped open.

"What's wrong? Who died?!"

"I'm late!"

"We don't have to go to work today, calm down."

My eyes narrowed, "Not late for work, stupid!"

She looked stumped for a moment and then gasped loudly, "Oh, hun! You're going to be a mommy!"

My stomach clenched, "I need Erik!"

"Well, let's get him! My car's outside." We ran out the door, pyjamas and all.

On the way to Erik's we passed a police car and I hesitated, slowing in the middle of the road.

"Is that . . . ?"

Cat nodded, "Yeah. It is."

"Should I follow?"

"I'd say you should."

I started to follow them but couldn't help feeling like something was going to happen. It wasn't until I saw Taylor coming to the intersection beside us that I knew I was right. What was he doing? I slammed on the brakes and watched him, praying that he was just driving to the store or something.

The last thing I remembered was watching Taylor laugh before he sped forward into the police car. It was right after that that my world crumbled into chaos. Screams pierced the air and brakes squealed, but all I heard was the sickening sound of metal crushing over and over in my head.

~*~

I woke up in a small white room with doctors hovering over me.

"Ms. Siykes, you're at the hospital," They explained. "You smacked your head on the steering wheel. From what we know, you don't have a concussion. We will have to monitor you for today, just to be sure."

My stomach whirled and I groaned, "Erik?"

The tall one on my right shuffled nervously, "Well . . . Ms. Siykes, he's stabilized, but I'm afraid he's in a coma."

Sobs broke out and wracked my body, "So, he's dead?"

"No. Not dead, just not . . . Living; sort of in the middle."

I felt anger boil up inside and I began to shout, "If the asshole responsible isn't locked up, I swear to God I'll kill him myself!"

The doctor's hands shot up in defense. "There's no reason for violence. You don't want to put stress on the baby. Taylor Guyon is safely behind bars until his trial."

I broke down again and began crying even more. "Will he ever come out of it? Can you save him?"

"The coma is induced Ms. Siykes, so as soon as his injuries have healed we can try to pull him out. It's completely up to him to wake up though."

"Can I see him?"

"Of course, if you'll just follow me." I was lead out of my room and down the corridor to the Trauma ward. "He's right in here."

Nodding, I walked hesitantly past him and into the room. A lifetime of ER shows could not have prepared me for what I saw inside. My beautiful, lively Erik was laid on a wheeled bed with bandages and tubes covering him.

"Ms. Siykes, Erik broke a total of 13 bones and suffered incredible damage to his skull. We repaired all that we could; those tubes are air, morphine-"

I cut him off with a sob. "Please stop."

Shakily, I stepped forward and wrapped my fingers gingerly around Erik's healing fingers. His skin was oddly pale underneath the purple bruises.

"Erik, I'm so sorry. I shouldn't have gotten so mad, this is all my fault."

I laid my head down next to his hand and cried myself into a fitful sleep.

CHAPTER TEN – OLIVIA

"The jury and I find you guilty on account of attempted murder, failing to withhold a restraining order and harassment. I hereby sentence you to fifteen years in prison and a monetary fine of two hundred fifty thousand dollars to be paid to Ms. Siykes to pay for hospital care." The gavel slammed down and I felt a weight lift off my shoulders. I was relieved that Erik was receiving justice and that my child would not be on the same streets with Taylor running rampant. However, simply putting Taylor behind bars wasn't going to revive Erik so he could be the father our child would need. Nor would it reverse the coma's effects on Erik's brain. I was told that even if Erik woke up, I'd probably spend somewhere around a year just trying to re-teach him all the things he'd now lost. I was nervous enough about having one person with no knowledge; I didn't know if I could handle two of them. Sighing, I exited the courtroom.

"Ms. Siykes! If you'll just excuse me for a moment!" An incredibly tanned man was walking swiftly towards me, hitting people with a large box that he held.

I stopped and waited for him to catch up, which took no time at all. "Can I help you?"

"Mr. Gorton told my partner and I that he wanted you to have everything. We had someone go through his belongings to see what you'd want right away. This is what she came up with; his keys are in there too, in case you wanted to get the rest of his stuff."

I blinked back the tears that had started to well up; didn't they know he wasn't dead? Why was everything being sorted through, he was going to wake up soon. If he loved me at all, he'd come back; I know it. None of that escaped my lips, though. I simply nodded and took the box from his hands.

He smiled apologetically, "I'm so sorry for your loss; Mr. Gorton told us the story of your sister's death and we're currently looking into it. The lie detector test stated that he was telling the truth, but we're going to ask around and find out who else was there."

"Thank you."

~*~

My composure diminished as soon as I got inside my house. I instantly began sobbing and hardly made it to the couch before my legs gave out, throwing me onto it. I clutched my swollen stomach and stared at the box of Erik's belongings. It was just a simple brown cardboard box, why was I so hesitant to touch it? Maybe it was that his stuff was inside, mocking me; I could have his things but I couldn't have him. What kind of sick joke was that? After wiping my eyes and taking a deep breath, I opened the box. On the top of the pile was a stack of photographs. Each and every picture had me in it, whether I was sitting around reading, sleeping or squished in the picture beside Erik. The very last one in the pile was a close up of Erik and I with our faces pressed together, smiling. The camera flash had perfectly illuminated our eyes, making us seem like polar opposites. Erik's honey coloured hair and sky blue eyes were so different than my own dark hair and jade green eyes. The hard lines around his always softened around me and this picture showed a perfect example of how everything could be forgotten in the correct company. I stared at the picture for an extra second before carefully placing it on the table in front of me. The next item in the box was a plain, black journal, which made me giggle a little. I would have never suspected Erik to have a journal; I clutched it close to my chest, knowing I held his most personal thoughts in my hands. A last look in the box showed a fluffy, white blanket, which I yanked out and wrapped around my shoulders. However, when I shoved the box off the couch, I heard a soft rattling sounds and picked it back up. Inside was a small, velvet box and inside that was a letter and a silver ring. I gasped and opened the letter first, leaving the ring in the box.

> *My dearest Olivia,*
>
> *If you're reading this then that means I was unable to give you this box myself. For whatever reason, whether it be that you're mad and I left this on your doorstep out of desperation or if I was sent to jail again, I just want you to know that I love you. Since the first day I saw you I knew that I would love you. I also wanted to tell you that I'm truly sorry for having to keep you in the dark for so long about my nightmares and the full story of my past. I promise that I'll tell you when I hear from you . . . Unless something has happened to me and in that case you should be receiving my journal. Inside that journal, you'll find my whole life. I wrote it all down, from A to Z. It's all there, just read it, Olivia. I think it will help you understand me better. So with that said, I just leave you with one question: will you marry me?*
>
> *Love for always,*
Erik
>
> *P.S. Cat called me; I want our baby's name to be either Alexander or Hanna.*

I nodded silently to the air around me and slipped the ring onto my finger.

CHAPTER ELEVEN

My body felt heavy, like my blood had been swapped with lead, Why was everything so damn heavy? I don't understand; my eyelashes were even weighted down, keeping me in the dark. Slowly, agonizingly so, I opened my eyes only to be blinded by white walls and sunlight. Groaning, I turned my head and saw a large machine that was continuously beeping. It annoyed me; the beeping became faster the more annoyed I got. Eventually it caught the attention of people walking outside the room because two girls dressed pink paper-y outfits came rushing in.

One of them looked at me and smiled, "Mr. Gorton, you've been in a coma for five months. You're in the hospital."

My tongue was thick with misuse when I answered, giving me a slur, "Mr. who? I don't understand."

The girls' faces were grim. "Do you remember anything at all?"

I shut my eyes, concentrating hard, and an entourage of pictures flashed through my head. A girl, always the same one, and me; we looked so happy. Then that girl was blonde and dead . . . no, different girl. Memories from my childhood-I assume they're mine anyways-were the easiest to see. I had an alcoholic mother, both my parents are dead, jail. Then I saw a car, it was speeding straight towards me . . .

Looking back up, I nodded, "I remember childhood, and jail, and a girl dying and another girl. The last girl and I, we were always together but I don't remember names."

They nodded again before the second one added, "We can begin therapy as soon as you're ready. That second girl, did she have dark hair?"

I nodded, "Yes, is she important?"

"That's Olivia, your fiancé."

" . . . Olivia."

*

I stayed in the hospital for another year and a half before a nurse came in with the best news I'd heard my whole life.

"Mr. Gorton, Olivia's here."

"Thank-you."

Quickly, I lay on the bed and braced myself to stay still no matter what. I needed to know if she still loved me.

CHAPTER TWELVE

It was two years later when I found the time and sensibility to re-visit Erik. Alexander hung on lightly to my arms, green eyes staring up at me with wonder.

"Mommy, are you shick?"

I looked down at him and smiled at his lisp, "No honey, we're going to see your daddy."

He looked down at his feet, concentrating on the stairs in front of him, "Is *he* shick?"

"Yes." I squeezed his hand lightly and looked at the sun glinting off his white hair. He reminded me so much of Erik; the way he moved, his hair, everything except his bright green eyes was Erik. Once inside the hospital, he stepped comically over the lines in the floor. We line jumped all the way to Erik's room where I calmed Alexander down with a hand on his shoulder. Instantly he settled down and silently followed me inside. Erik's once purple and bandaged body was now healed and pale. The doctors told me they had tried three times to pull him from his coma but he still wouldn't wake up. I wrapped my fingers around Erik's tightly, now un-afraid of damaging healing bones, and reminisced about everything we'd had before the day of the crash.

"Mommy, ish that my daddy?"

I swallowed the lump in my throat, "Yes, this is your daddy."

He looked at Erik for a moment before running around the other side of the bed and clambering onto a chair. "He looksh jusht like me!" Alexander beamed at me while he crawled onto the bed to snuggle into Erik's side.

I laughed a little, "Yeah, he does. Except you have my eyes."

"What color are Daddy'sh eyesh?"

"Blue, like the sky. You could always tell what was going on by what his eyes looked like, because they got dark when he was upset, just like storm clouds." It didn't sound as good as I had hoped, but I wanted Alexander to know things about his father. Little things that could be used to remember him, like how his eyes resembled the sky or how he could walk around without making a sound. Alexander nodded and nuzzled into Erik's side again.

I bent down and kissed Erik's forehead before whispering in his ear, "Erik, wake up please. Your son needs his father and I need my fiancé." No reaction, just silence. Two years of silence. I blinked back tears and motioned to Alexander that it was time to say good-bye. I knew this was the last time we would come see Erik, I had decided to let him go. There was no point in keeping his body alive if his brain was dead. Alexander smiled at me, climbed off the bed and left to stand in the hallway. I was left to say my final good-bye.

"Erik, you were right about Antonio; he killed Mae, not you. You're a free man. I love you Erik, always have and always will."

I sniffed and wiped the tears off my face before leaving the room. When I tried to grab Alexander's hand, he shook me off and ran back inside. Shrugging, I admired children's drawings on the walls and hummed to myself. I was trying to decipher green scribbles when I heard peals of laughter coming from Erik's room. Quickly running inside, I found Alexander lying on the bed beside Erik, laughing.

"Alexander, what's so funny?"

"He tickled me!"

I frowned, "he couldn't have tickled you."

"Show her Daddy!"

Then, just like magic, Erik's hand fluttered across Alexander's belly. However, I was watching two bright blue eyes open and blink. Just in case I wasn't surprised enough, he spoke.

Without a hint of lost memory, he told me what I had longed to hear for two years, "I love you too."

EPILOGUE

It's Alexander's first day of school. He grinned up at me, showing off his missing front tooth. The same tooth that brought back the lisp he had previously outgrew.

"I'm ready for shcool!"

"Okay, do you want me to walk you to the bus stop?" I already knew the answer, but I had to ask anyways. That's part of being a father, being responsible.

"No! I can go by myshelf Daddy!"

I smiled and ruffled his hair into a white nest on the top of his head. Laughing, he ran to the door and opened it to look outside. The leaves outside hadn't yet begun to change colors but the cold air made sure we all knew it was fall. Time for the death of old and the birth of new. Time to-

"Daddy! Can you jusht watch me?"

I nodded, "Of course I can."

Smiling, he stepped out the door. Stepped out to a new town where we could live in peace without being bogged down by memories. Speaking of which, I'd regained all those memories with Olivia's help. I also no longer woke up screaming and shaking. In fact, I hadn't had a nightmare since I left the hospital. That was definitely the best part of having been in a coma. All those things that my brain kept dredging up had been released. No longer weighted down by those, I was able to resume a happy life with my now wife and son. From the edge of the driveway I could see Alexander waving to me; I waved back silently before I felt a pair of hands slide around my abdomen. Smiling to myself, I laid my hands on top of her small, clasped ones.

Olivia nuzzled into my shoulder and watched Alexander board the bus through the windowed door before questioning my silence, "What are you thinking?"

"I'm just thinking about how happy I am with you, and how glad I am that you decided to visit me that time, and how I just want to pause time and stay like this forever."

"We're thinking the same thing then . . ."

I turned her slowly so I could kiss her forehead. "I love you, Olivia."

"I love you too Erik."

"Always have . . ."

"Always will . . ."

Want to know Taylor's thoughts?
If so, read on . . .

#1

    I've been watching. Ever since she told me that I had no right to. I don't like rules. I know that she's been seeing some blonde pretty boy. He showed up out of the blue and stole her attention from me. That's when I became a shadow; lurking in the dark and learning everything I could. Now, I know that I sound like a stalker. But I'm not! She's mine! Olivia is mine! Not some guy she just met! I need to talk to her! Just my luck, here she is.

"Olivia."

Her footsteps faltered, "what do you want?"

"You know what I want." I wrapped my fingers around her wrist, attempting to contain her.

However, she shook me off and began to run. *You're not getting off that easy Olivia.* I chased her. I chased her all the way past that pretty boy, Erik.

#2

    He broke my nose. Gruffly, I reached up and cracked it back into place. The crack it made was sickening and I groaned. I swear, he won't live for much longer. That pretty boy is going to pay for breaking my nose and stealing my girl. I'm going to dig up enough dirt to fill his grave.

#3

He's a felon! That pretty boy killed Olivia's sister and spent 10 years in jail! Oh, this is going to be good . . .

#4

    Erik has struck again! A man was found dead this morning with the same type of knife in his stomach! He must be a serial killer! What if Olivia's next? He cannot be trusted. I'm contacting detectives.

#5

The looks on their faces were priceless! I feel like singing. However, the detectives and I were sent away. This is going to take more than I thought. I'm sure he's feeling the heat . . . . I need him to stop feeling.

#6

    This is my chance. He's in the cop car. I can see him. Today, Erik Gorton dies.

#7

He's not dead! I only put him in a coma. Damnit! Well, that's better than alive I guess. Except now I'm going to jail. Damn you Olivia! This is all your fault. When I get out, I will find you. You and Erik will pay for this. I swear.